THE
Jewel
Fairies
COLLECTION

Volume 1
BOOKS #1-4

THE Jewel Fairies

COLLECTION

Volume 1
BOOKS #1-4

by Daisy Meadows

SCHOLASTIC INC.

New York   Toronto   London   Auckland   Sydney
Mexico City   New Delhi   Hong Kong   Buenos Aires

No part of this publication may be reproduced, stored in a retrieval system, or transmitted in any form or by any means, electronic, mechanical, photocopying, recording, or otherwise, without written permission of the publisher. For information regarding permission, write to Rainbow Magic Limited c/o HIT Entertainment, 830 South Greenville Avenue, Allen, TX 75002-3320.

Jewel Fairies #1: India the Moonstone Fairy, ISBN 0-439-93528-8
Jewel Fairies #2: Scarlett the Garnet Fairy, ISBN 0-439-93529-6
Jewel Fairies #3: Emily the Emerald Fairy, ISBN 0-439-93530-X
Jewel Fairies #4: Chloe the Topaz Fairy, ISBN 0-439-93531-8

These books were originally published in the U.S.A. by Little Apple Paperbacks.

ISBN-13: 978-0-545-08838-1
ISBN-10: 0-545-08838-0

12 11 10 9 8 7 6 5 4 3 2 1   8 9 10 11 12 13/0

Printed in the U.S.A.   40

This collection first printing, May 2008

This special collection includes the
following four books!

Contents

The Fairyland Palace

Adventure Playground

Tippington Manor

Tippington Town

The Tall Toy Store

Fountain

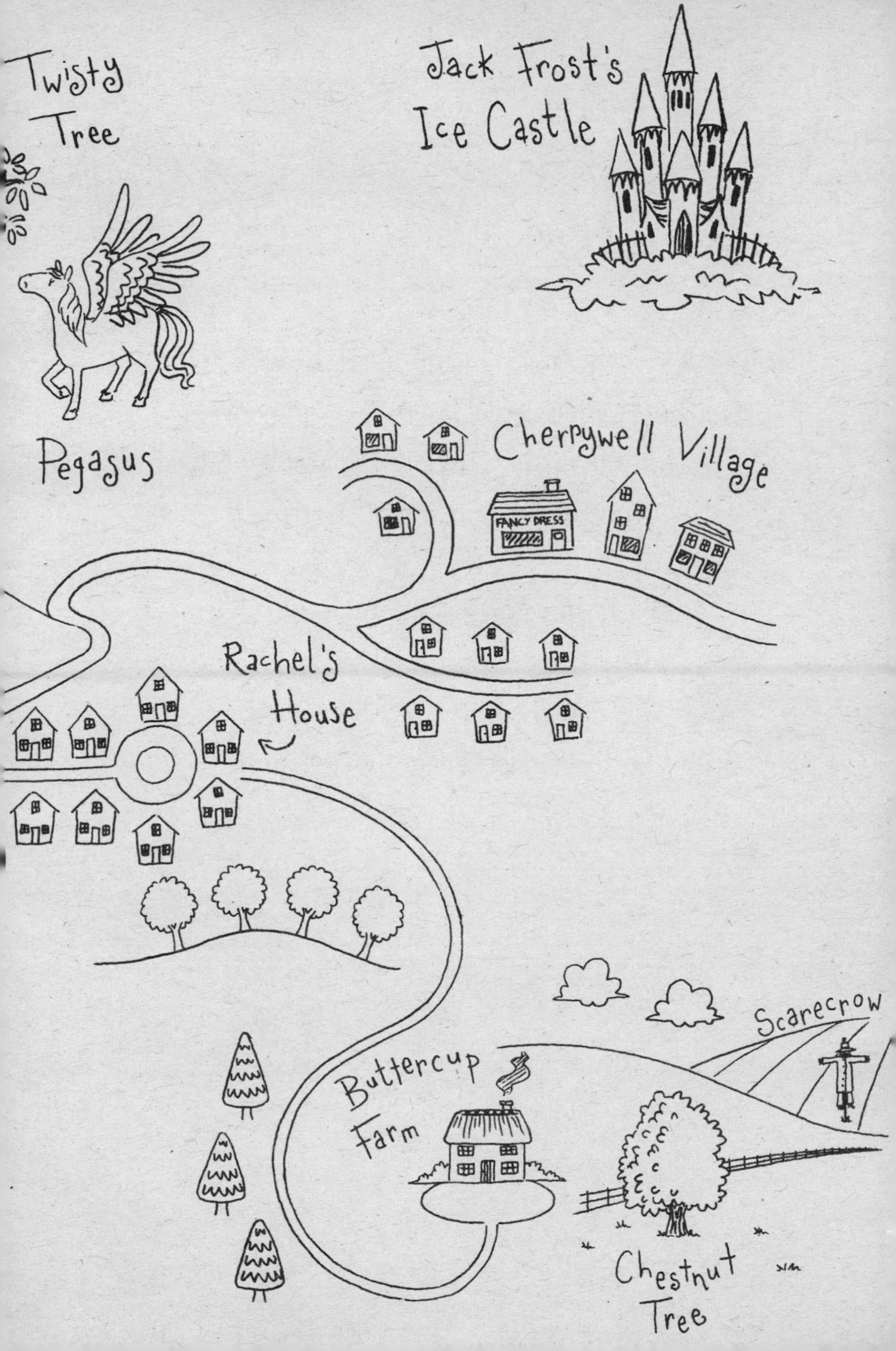

Twisty Tree

Jack Frost's Ice Castle

Pegasus

Cherrywell Village

FANCY DRESS

Rachel's House

Buttercup Farm

Scarecrow

Chestnut Tree

By frosty magic I cast away
These seven jewels with their fiery rays,
So their magic powers will not be felt
And my icy castle shall not melt.

The fairies may search high and low
To find the gems and take them home.
But I will send my goblin guards
To make the fairies' mission hard.

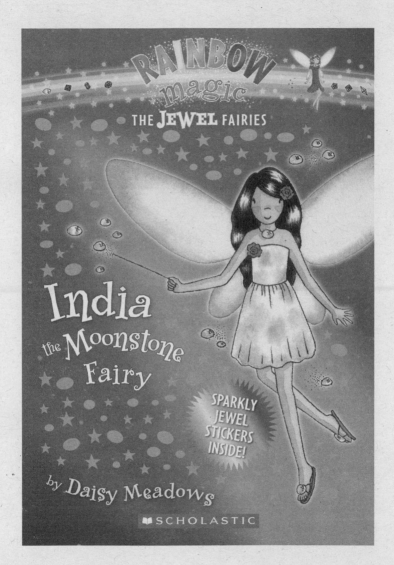

RAINBOW magic

THE JEWEL FAIRIES

India
the Moonstone Fairy

SPARKLY JEWEL STICKERS INSIDE!

by Daisy Meadows

SCHOLASTIC

For Danni, who loves fairies

Special thanks to
Narinder Dhami

A Nasty Nightmare

"Kirsty, help!" Rachel Walker shouted. "The goblins are going to get me!"

Breathing hard, Rachel glanced behind her. She was running as fast as she could, but the green goblins were getting closer and closer. They were grinning nastily, showing their pointed teeth. Now one of them had grabbed Rachel by the shoulder and was shaking her —

"Rachel?" Kirsty Tate was leaning over her friend's bed, trying to awaken her. "Wake up! You're having a nightmare."

Rachel sat up in bed. "What time is it?" she asked. "I had a dream that there were horrible goblins chasing me and I couldn't get away."

"It's seven thirty," Kirsty replied, sitting on the edge of the bed. "Why were the goblins after you in your dream?"

Rachel frowned. "I can't remember," she said, sighing. "But you know what, Kirsty? I have a funny feeling that Jack Frost might be causing trouble again!"

Kirsty eyes opened wide. "Do you really think so?" She gasped. "Then maybe our fairy friends need our help!"

Rachel and Kirsty shared a magical  secret. They had become friends with the fairies! Whenever there was a problem in Fairyland, Kirsty and Rachel were asked to help.

The fairies' biggest enemy was Jack Frost. He and his mean goblins were always causing problems. Not long ago, Jack Frost had mixed up all the weather in Fairyland. But luckily, Kirsty and Rachel had come to the rescue.

"We'll have to keep our eyes open," Rachel agreed. "If the fairies need our help, they'll let us know somehow."

Kirsty nodded. "Well, it's only the beginning of our school break, and I'm staying with you for the whole week," she pointed out. "So we have lots of time."

Before Rachel could reply, she felt a gentle tug at her neck. Both she and Kirsty jumped.

"What was that?" Kirsty asked.

Rachel looked at her friend. "You felt it, too?" Rachel looked down and gasped. The locket around her neck was glowing! "Look, Kirsty!" she cried. "Your locket is glowing, too!"

Rachel and Kirsty took a closer look at their necklaces. Rachel was right! The lockets were glowing with a faint pink light.

After helping the Weather Fairies stop Jack Frost from mixing up the weather in Fairyland, Rachel and Kirsty had each been given a beautiful locket. The lockets were filled with fairy dust, and the girls wore them every day. But they had never glowed like this before! What could it mean? There was only one way to find out. The girls were pretty sure that another fairy adventure wasn't far away!

"Let's open them, Rachel," Kirsty whispered.

Holding their breath, both girls slowly pried open their lockets.

Immediately, a glittering shower of multicolored fairy dust burst from both lockets. It swirled around the girls, wrapping them in a cloud of sparkles and lifting them off their feet.

Fairy News

After a minute or two, the sparkles began
to fade. Rachel and Kirsty felt their feet
lightly touch the ground. They blinked a
few times and looked around.

"Kirsty, we're in Fairyland!" Rachel
gasped.

"In our pajamas!" Kirsty added.

The girls were fairy-size and had

glittering fairy wings on their backs!
They were standing in the golden Great
Hall of the fairy palace. King Oberon,
Queen Titania, and a small crowd of
fairies stood in front of them. The girls
noticed that all of the fairies looked very
worried.

Queen Titania stepped forward.
"Welcome back, girls," she said with a
smile. "I hope you don't mind us
bringing you here without warning."

"Of course not," Rachel said quickly.

"You have been such good friends to us in the past," the queen went on. "We were hoping you might be able to help us again. I'm afraid that we are in trouble."

"What's wrong?" asked Kirsty.

"Let me explain," the queen replied sadly. "Every year, at Halloween, we have a huge celebration in Fairyland. That's when all the fairies recharge their fairy magic for another year."

"Every fairy in Fairyland parades around the Grand Square," King Oberon added. "Then they all march into the palace, where Queen Titania's crown rests upon a velvet pillow."

"It sounds wonderful," Rachel said. She hoped that she and Kirsty would be allowed to watch the parade one day.

Queen Titania nodded. "It is," she replied. "And my crown is a very important part of fairy magic. It contains seven beautiful jewels. A sparkling fountain of fairy dust pours from each of the seven jewels, and they join together to form a great, glittering rainbow."

Kirsty and Rachel listened carefully, their eyes wide. "What happens then?" Kirsty asked.

"Each fairy must recharge her wand by dipping it in the rainbow," the queen explained. "Then she will be able to perform magic for another year."

The king shook his head sadly. "But now Jack Frost has ended all that," he said, sighing. "Two nights ago, he crept into the palace and stole the seven jewels from Queen Titania's crown!"

"Oh, no!" Rachel and Kirsty exclaimed together.

"Our special celebration is only a week away," the queen went on, looking worried. "So the fairies' magic is already running low."

"The jewels must be returned to the crown before the Jewel Fairies run out of magic completely!" King Oberon added.

"Does this mean that there will be no magic at all left in Fairyland?" asked Kirsty anxiously.

"Not exactly," the queen replied. "Fairy magic is more complicated than that. Some magic, like Weather Magic and Rainbow Magic, isn't controlled by the jewels."

"But the jewels do control some of the most important kinds of fairy magic," the king added. "They are in charge of things like flying, wishes, and sweet dreams. Some people have already started to have nightmares!"

Rachel nodded, thinking about her own scary dream. "We have to get the jewels back!" she said firmly.

"Where is Jack Frost now?" Kirsty asked. "Did he take the jewels to his ice castle?"

The queen shook her head. "Jack Frost doesn't have the jewels anymore," she said. "Come with us. We will show you what happened."

Rachel and Kirsty followed the fairies outside to the beautiful palace gardens. They stopped next to the golden pool. Its surface was as clear and smooth as glass.

"Watch," Queen Titania said softly, waving her wand over the water.

Immediately, tiny ripples spread across the surface of the pool. The ripples grew bigger and bigger, and a picture slowly appeared in the water.

"It's Jack Frost!" Rachel cried.
Tall, thin Jack Frost stood in
front of Queen Titania's
golden crown. The
seven magic jewels
glittered as streams
of magic dust
poured from
them. Laughing,
Jack Frost thrust
his wand into
the magic
rainbow, where
it glowed
like fire.
"He is
recharging his
magic," King
Oberon explained.

Kirsty and Rachel watched in dismay as Jack Frost pulled the sparkling gems out of the crown. He waved his wand, and immediately the jewels were surrounded by ice.

"What is he doing?" Rachel asked, confused.

"The light and heat of the jewels'
magic makes them
difficult for cold
creatures like
Jack Frost
and his
goblins to
hold," Queen
Titania explained.
Now Jack
Frost was
flying back to
his ice castle,
carried by a frosty
wind. He held the jewels in his arms, but
Rachel and Kirsty could see that the ice

around them was already beginning to melt.

Jack Frost swooped down from the gray sky and landed in his ice castle. By now, the ice around the jewels was almost gone. The jewels glowed, casting shimmering rays of light into every corner of the icy room. Goblins came running to see the gems. They wore sunglasses to protect their eyes from the light.

"Stand back, you fools!" Jack Frost roared, waving his wand and casting another spell to cover the jewels with ice. But the jewels were still glowing, and the ice began to melt away.

"Look, Master!" yelled one of the goblins. "The fairy magic is melting your castle!"

Jack Frost looked around in rage. Sure enough, water was beginning to trickle

down the icy walls, and there was a huge puddle at the foot of his ice throne.

"Jack Frost's magic is not strong enough to block the power of the jewels," Queen Titania told Rachel and Kirsty.

The girls watched as the goblins began rushing around, mopping up the water as fast as they could. But as soon as they

soaked up one puddle, two more
appeared.

"Fine!" shouted Jack Frost, stomping
his feet in anger. "If I cannot keep the
magic jewels, no one else can have them,
either! I will cast a spell to get rid of
them." And he raised his wand high
above his head.

Lost!

"Oh, no!" Kirsty gasped. She and
Rachel watched in horror as a chilly
blast of wind tore through the ice
castle. The glowing jewels were sent
spinning out of the window, where they
scattered.

"See how the jewels grow larger as

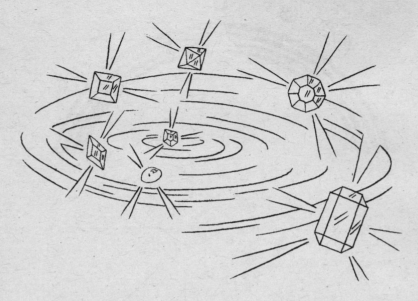

they fall into the human world?" Queen
Titania pointed out. The image in the
pool began to flicker and fade. "Because
they are magical, the jewels will hide
themselves until we can find them and
bring them back to Fairyland."

The picture in the pool was fading fast.
But just before it disappeared, Rachel
saw one of the jewels, a cream-colored

stone, fall into someone's backyard. Rachel was surprised to realize that she knew exactly whose yard it was!

Queen Titania shook her head sadly as the image vanished. "All of our fairy seeing magic is used up," she said, sighing. "The pool can't show us where all the jewels have gone."

"But I know where one of them is!" Rachel burst out excitedly. "I recognized the yard where it fell!"

Everyone turned to stare at her.

"Are you sure, Rachel?" Kirsty asked.

Rachel nodded. "It was Mr. and Mrs. Palmer's backyard," she explained.

"The Palmers are my parents' friends. I've been to their house lots of times to help my mom babysit their little girl, Ellie."

One of the fairies was so excited to hear this that she whirled up into the air. Her long brown hair streamed out behind her. "I'm India the Moonstone Fairy," she cried, her eyes shining. "And I'm sure it was my moonstone that fell into your friends' backyard!"

The little fairy wore a pretty dress with a fluttery skirt. The dress was white, but every time India moved, Rachel and Kirsty could see shimmering flashes of pink and blue.

On her feet, India wore dainty white
sandals.

"You must meet all our Jewel Fairies,"
said King Oberon as the other fairies
crowded around. "Each one is responsible
for teaching all the other fairies in
Fairyland how to use her jewel's magic."
He pointed at India the Moonstone
Fairy. "India teaches dream magic, while
Scarlett the Garnet Fairy teaches
growing and shrinking magic, Emily
the Emerald Fairy teaches seeing
magic, Chloe the Topaz Fairy teaches
changing and transforming magic, Amy
the Amethyst Fairy teaches appearing
and disappearing magic, Sophie the
Sapphire Fairy teaches wishing magic,
and Lucy the Diamond Fairy teaches
flying magic."

Rachel and Kirsty smiled at all the
Jewel Fairies. "We'll do our best to get
your jewels back," Kirsty said.

"Thank you," the fairies replied.

"We knew you would help us," Queen
Titania said gratefully. "But Jack Frost
knows we will be trying to find the
jewels, too. He has sent his goblins into
the human world to guard them."

"The goblins will have trouble picking up the jewels," King Oberon continued. "The bright light and magic of the gems will burn them, because goblins belong to the cold, icy world of Jack Frost. Instead, the goblins will probably hide near the jewels and try to keep us from getting them back."

Rachel and Kirsty nodded. They weren't eager to see the goblins again, but they had to help their fairy friends!

Queen Titania looked serious. "So we not only need your help to find each magic jewel," she said, "but to outwit the goblins that are guarding them!"

On the Right Track

"We'll find a way to get the jewels back," Rachel said firmly. Kirsty nodded.

King Oberon smiled at them. "And you will have our Jewel Fairies to help you."

Rachel frowned. "I had a dream that the goblins were chasing me," she said slowly.

India sighed, looking
very sad. "Without
the moonstone, the
fairies' power to
send sweet dreams
into the human
world is fading," she
explained. "That's
why you had a nightmare, Rachel."

"India will return with you to your
world," said Queen Titania. "She'll help
you find the moonstone."

"We know we have to look in the
Palmers' backyard," Kirsty said. "But
how will we know where to search for
the other jewels?"

Queen Titania smiled. "You must let
the magic come to you," she replied.
"The jewels will find you! And

remember, they have grown bigger in
the human world, so they will be easier
to spot."

Rachel and Kirsty nodded. Then India
fluttered over to join them. The Fairy
Queen raised her wand.

"Good luck!" called the fairies. Queen
Titania waved her wand, and Rachel,
Kirsty, and India disappeared in a shower
of magic sparkles.

When the cloud of fairy dust had vanished, Rachel and Kirsty realized that they were back in Rachel's bedroom.

"We must get to work right away, girls!" called a silvery voice.

The girls turned and saw India perched on top of Rachel's mirror.

"Yes, let's go over to the Palmers' house now," said Rachel eagerly. She headed for the door.

Suddenly, Kirsty burst out laughing. "I think we'd better change out of our pajamas first, don't you?"

"Good idea!" Rachel grinned.

"How will we get into the Palmers' backyard?" India asked as the girls quickly got dressed.

"We could throw a ball over the fence," Kirsty suggested. "Then we could ask the Palmers to let us into their yard to find it."

"Yes, that would work," Rachel agreed.

"Girls, are you awake?" Mrs. Walker's voice drifted up the stairs. "Breakfast is ready."

India fluttered across the room and hid  herself in Kirsty's pocket, and the girls hurried downstairs. "Mom," said Rachel as she and Kirsty ate toast and cereal, "is it OK if we go out to play after breakfast?"

"Sure," Mrs. Walker agreed. "But don't go farther than the park, and be back in time for lunch."

"Thanks, Mom!" Rachel said, getting up out of her chair.

Kirsty did the same. "We need a ball," she whispered as they headed outside.

"There's one in the shed, I think," Rachel replied.

The girls found a tennis ball and headed down the street. Even though it was autumn, it was a warm day. The sun shone down brightly from the blue sky.

"I hope my moonstone is safe," India said softly, popping her head out of Kirsty's pocket. "I wonder if there are any goblins guarding it."

"We'll find out soon," Rachel replied, stopping in front of a house with a bright red door. "This is the Palmers' house."

The house was only three doors down from Rachel's, on the corner of the street. Rachel took the ball out of her pocket, slipped around the corner, and tossed it

over the fence into the backyard. Then
she joined Kirsty and India again in front
of the house.

"I'll knock on the door," Rachel said,
leading the way up the front steps.

"Let's hope they're
home!" replied Kirsty.

Rachel rang the
bell, but everything
was quiet for a while.
Just as the girls and
India were starting to
give up hope, the
door opened.

"Hello, Rachel,"
said Mrs. Palmer,
smiling. "And this
must be Kirsty. Rachel told me
she was having a friend visit this week."

"It's nice to meet you," Kirsty said
politely.

"Sorry to disturb you, Mrs. Palmer,"
Rachel said, "but I'm afraid we just lost
our ball in your backyard."

Mrs. Palmer smiled. "As a matter of
fact, I was just sitting out back with Ellie.
I didn't see your ball. Do you want to
come and look for it?"

"Yes, please," Rachel replied.

"If you don't mind,"
added Kirsty.

Mrs. Palmer
opened the door
wide. "Go right
through, girls. I'm
just going to run
upstairs for a
minute. Ellie's

in her stroller on the patio, if you want to say hello."

Rachel led Kirsty through the kitchen and out the back door.

India popped her head out of Kirsty's pocket. "The moonstone is here somewhere," she cried happily. "I can feel it!"

"It's a big yard," Kirsty said. "We'd better start looking right away."

She and India hurried over to the nearest flowerbed and began to look through the shrubs. Meanwhile,

Rachel went across the patio to say hello to Ellie. But as she walked toward the stroller, Rachel began to shiver. Suddenly, there was a chill in the air.

A loud wail came from the stroller as Ellie started to cry.

Ellie must be feeling the cold, too! Rachel thought. *But it was warm just a minute ago!*

Mrs. Palmer rushed out of the house and ran over to the stroller. "It's very strange, Rachel," she said. She pushed back the shade and bent down to pick up the baby. "Ellie's always had trouble sleeping. Then yesterday, we got this mobile for her stroller, and she's been sleeping so well." Mrs. Palmer frowned, lifting Ellie out from under her blanket. "Something seems to be upsetting her today, though. She's been restless all morning."

As Mrs. Palmer picked up Ellie, the baby stretched out her chubby little hand to grab one of the decorations hanging from the mobile. Rachel looked at the mobile more closely. It was hung with silver stars, yellow suns, and pale moons. And then, suddenly, her heart skipped a beat. There, glittering in the middle of the mobile, was a cream-colored stone that flashed with pink-and-blue light.

The moonstone! Rachel thought excitedly. *No wonder Ellie's been sleeping well. She must have had extra-sweet dreams!*

"I'm going to take Ellie inside, but feel free to keep looking for your ball," said Mrs. Palmer. "I don't want Ellie to catch a cold. It's a little chilly all of a sudden."

I hope that doesn't mean that some of Jack Frost's goblins are nearby, Rachel thought.

As Mrs. Palmer turned to go inside with Ellie, Rachel ran across the grass

toward Kirsty and India. They were searching around the birdbath in the middle of the yard.

"I found the moonstone!" Rachel whispered triumphantly. "It's hanging in the middle of the mobile on Ellie's stroller."

"Wonderful!" India gasped.

"Way to go, Rachel!" added Kirsty.

"Mrs. Palmer's taking Ellie inside," said Rachel. "We can get the moonstone as soon as she's gone."

The girls and India watched as Mrs. Palmer carried Ellie into the house. Then Rachel and Kirsty immediately ran toward the stroller. India flew along beside them. But before they reached it, the door of the garden shed crashed open, and two green goblins rushed out!

The Big Chase

"The moonstone is ours!" one of the goblins yelled. "We'll never let the fairies have it back!"

"Never! Never!" shouted the other goblin.

As Kirsty, Rachel, and India watched in horror, the second goblin jumped up onto the stroller and grabbed the mobile.

"He's going to take the moonstone!"
Rachel gasped. "Stop him!"

As the girls rushed toward the stroller,
the other goblin panicked. He rushed to
push the stroller away from the girls.

But the stroller was
much bigger than
the goblin, who
was only knee-
high. He couldn't
control it!
The stroller
bumped and
bounced over
the grass. The goblin
inside was caught off-balance! With a
screech of rage, he tumbled over and got
tangled in the baby's blankets before he
could grab the moonstone.

Kirsty, Rachel, and India chased after the goblin as he charged across the grass, pushing the stroller in front of him. They could see the moonstone swinging wildly on the mobile, but they couldn't reach it. The goblins were too far ahead!

The stroller jolted along, while the goblin inside struggled to free himself from the tangle of blankets. He shouted at his friend to stop, but with no luck.

Then, all of a sudden, one wheel hit a large stone lying in the middle of the yard. The stroller was moving so quickly that it flipped over! Both goblins let out cries of alarm as they flew through the air. They landed in a heap underneath a large pine tree, covered by Ellie's blankets.

"India, can you keep them from getting away?" Kirsty panted as she and

Rachel ran across the
yard toward the
goblins.

"I only have a little
dream magic left. It
might be enough to
put the goblins to
sleep," India replied.
She flew ahead of
the girls and hovered over
the goblins, waving her
wand. A few sparkles of fairy
dust drifted down. The goblins
stopped struggling to free themselves and
began yawning and rubbing their eyes
instead.

"I'm so tired!" one of them said with
a sigh.

"And this blanket is really warm and cozy," the other one said sleepily. "I think I might take a little nap."

"Me, too," the first goblin agreed. "Sing me a lullaby."

"No, *you* sing a lullaby!" the second goblin demanded.

"No, YOU!" yelled the first.

"They're waking themselves up with

their silly argument!" Rachel exclaimed.
"What are we going to do?"

"I think I have an idea!" Kirsty
whispered. Without saying anything else,
she hurried toward the goblins.

Rock-a-bye, Goblins

Rachel and India watched as Kirsty walked right up to the goblins and began to tuck them into the blankets.

"Now, now, settle down," she said in a soft, sweet voice. "It's time for your nap."

The goblins stopped arguing and started yawning again.

"I *am* sleepy," the first goblin mumbled, snuggling down under the pink blanket.

But the second goblin was trying hard to keep his eyes open. "Isn't there something we were supposed to do?" he asked.

Rachel hurried over to help Kirsty. "Go to sleep now," she said in a soothing voice. "You can worry about that later."

Then Kirsty began to sing a lullaby to the tune of "Rock-a-bye, Baby":

"Rock-a-bye, Goblins, under a tree,
out in the backyard, sleeping with glee.
When you wake up from your little nap,
you'll find that India has her stone back."

By the second line of Kirsty's song, both goblins were snoring loudly.

"Nice job, Kirsty," Rachel said with a grin. "But we can't leave the goblins here for Mrs. Palmer to find!"

"Leave that to me," India chimed in. She waved her wand over a large branch of the pine tree. Immediately, the branch drooped lower, so that it completely covered the sleeping goblins.

"Perfect!" Kirsty declared. "The goblins are green like the leaves, so they'll be well hidden until they wake up."

India and Rachel laughed.

"Then they'll have to go back to Jack Frost and tell him they lost the moonstone," India said. "They'll be in big trouble!"

Chuckling quietly, the girls picked up the stroller and pushed it back to the patio. Then, as India watched happily, Kirsty carefully took the moonstone from the middle of the mobile. It flashed and gleamed in the sunlight.

"We can't ruin Ellie's mobile," India said. She waved her wand, and a glittering, shiny bubble appeared in place of the moonstone.

As it caught the light, it sent rainbow colors sparkling in all directions.

"And now," India went on, "the moonstone is going right back to Fairyland and Queen Titania's crown, where it belongs!" She touched her wand to the jewel. Immediately, a fountain of

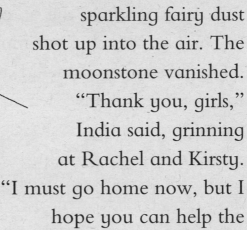

sparkling fairy dust shot up into the air. The moonstone vanished. "Thank you, girls," India said, grinning at Rachel and Kirsty. "I must go home now, but I hope you can help the other Jewel Fairies find their magic jewels, too."

"We'll do our best!" Rachel promised.

"Good-bye, India!" Kirsty added as their fairy friend flew away in a cloud of sparkles.

"I wonder where the six other jewels are hiding," Rachel murmured.

"And I wonder if we'll have to face many more goblins," Kirsty said with a frown.

Rachel shivered, remembering her nightmare. "I just hope I don't dream about them again tonight," she said.

Kirsty laughed. "Don't worry, Rachel," she told her friend. "India has the moonstone back now. And you helped her find it. She's sure to send you sweet dreams!"

RAINBOW magic™

THE JEWEL FAIRIES

Scarlett the Garnet Fairy

SPARKLY JEWEL STICKERS INSIDE!

by Daisy Meadows

■ SCHOLASTIC

To Josephine Scarlet Whitehouse
— a little jewel, herself

Special thanks to
Sue Mongredien

A Walk on the Farm

"Time to get up!" Rachel Walker called, bouncing on the end of her friend Kirsty's bed. Kirsty Tate was staying with the Walker family during their school break, and Rachel didn't want to waste a single second.

Kirsty yawned and stretched. "I just had the best dream," she said sleepily.

"Queen Titania asked us to help the
Jewel Fairies find seven stolen gemstones
from her magic crown, and . . ." Her
voice trailed away and she opened
her eyes wide. "It wasn't a dream, was
it?" she said, sitting up in bed. "We
really *did* meet India the Moonstone
Fairy yesterday!"

Rachel nodded, smiling. "Yes, we did,"
she agreed.

Kirsty and Rachel shared a wonderful secret. They were friends with the fairies! They had had all sorts of wonderful adventures with them in the past — but now the fairies were in trouble.

Mean Jack Frost had stolen the seven magical jewels from the Fairy Queen's crown. He had tried to keep the jewels for himself, but their magic was so powerful that his ice castle had started to melt. In a rage, Jack Frost had thrown the jewels far away into the human world. Now they were lost.

King Oberon and Queen Titania had asked Rachel and Kirsty to help return the jewels to Fairyland. The day before, the girls had helped India the Moonstone Fairy find the magic moonstone. But there were still six jewels left to find!

"I'm glad the moonstone is safely back in Fairyland," Rachel said. "And I had a great dream last night, so we know for sure that India's dream magic is working again."

The Fairy King and Queen had told the girls all about the jewels from Queen Titania's crown. They controlled some of the most important kinds of fairy magic. Every year, in a special ceremony, the fairies would recharge their magic by dipping their wands in the magical rainbow that streamed from the crown. But Jack Frost had stolen the jewels right before this year's ceremony. And that meant all the fairies were running low on a lot of their special magic.

"We have to track down the other

jewels before the fairies' magic is gone,"
Kirsty said, getting dressed quickly.
"Maybe we'll find another jewel today!"

Rachel agreed, and together the girls
hurried downstairs for breakfast.
Unfortunately, it
drizzled all morning.
There was no sign of
any jewels or any
fairies! After lunch,
though, the clouds
cleared to reveal a
blue sky and sunshine.

"Who wants to
come with me to Buttercup Farm?" Mrs.
Walker asked, clearing the lunch table.
"We need some vegetables and
eggs — and you two look like you could
use some fresh air."

"We could!" Rachel agreed, grinning at Kirsty. She held up crossed fingers while her mom wasn't looking. "Maybe we'll find another jewel," she added in a whisper.

A few minutes later, the girls and Mrs. Walker headed down the street toward the farm. Buttons, the Walkers' dog, trotted happily alongside them, sniffing

at interesting smells on the side of
the road.

"He loves going to the
farm," Rachel told
Kirsty, patting
Buttons. "He's
known the
Johnsons'
sheepdog,
Cloud, since
they were
both
puppies. The
two of them go
crazy whenever
they see each other. Don't you, boy?"

Woof! barked Buttons, as if he agreed
with her.

As the girls walked behind Mrs. Walker, something caught Kirsty's eye. "Look at those," she said, pointing to some red-and-white toadstools under a nearby tree. "They're exactly like the Fairyland toadstool houses, aren't they?" Rachel nodded. "Oh, I hope we meet another fairy today, Kirsty!" she said.

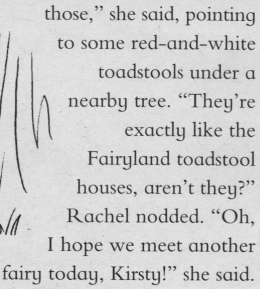

Kirsty crunched through the fallen leaves. "You know what Queen Titania always says," she whispered as Mrs. Walker bent down and let Buttons off his leash. "Don't go looking for magic . . ."

"It will find you!" Rachel finished.

Kirsty linked her arm through Rachel's. "It is hard not to look, though," she confessed. "I keep wondering where we're going to meet our next fairy — and who it's going to be!"

"Here we are," Mrs. Walker said as they turned onto a long driveway.

An old stone farmhouse stood up ahead. It had a pretty thatched roof and smoke curling from the chimney.

A smiling woman opened the front door. "Hello," she called warmly. "Come in, all of you. Oh, Buttons, too! Cloud will be so happy to see him."

"This is my friend Kirsty. She's staying with us," Rachel said. "And Kirsty, this is Mrs. Johnson."

"Hello," Kirsty said, returning Mrs. Johnson's smile.

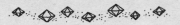

"Nice to meet you, Kirsty," Mrs. Johnson said, leading the way into the sunny farmhouse kitchen. "I just picked the last few plums from my plum tree. Would anyone like one?"

"Yes, please!" the girls replied.

A chorus of barks greeted them in the kitchen. Cloud, a black-and-white sheepdog, danced around their legs. Buttons ran joyfully after him, barking just as loudly.

"Should we take the dogs for a walk?" Rachel offered as Buttons's tail almost knocked over a basket of eggs.

"Good idea," Mrs. Johnson replied, giving each girl a handful of plums. "Oh!" she added as they were about to head out the door. "I should warn you that Mr.

Johnson is in a pretty bad mood. His new tractor disappeared, and he thinks one of the farm boys took it for a ride." She winked at the girls. "So if you see him and he seems grumpy, don't take it personally."

The girls nodded and followed Buttons and Cloud out into the meadow. Suddenly, Cloud trotted back over to the girls, looking very pleased with

himself. He dropped something at
their feet.

"What's this?" Kirsty asked, bending to
pick it up. "Oh, look, Rachel!" she said.
"It's a tiny toy tractor." She giggled. "Do
you think we should give it to Mr.
Johnson to make up for the one he lost?"

Rachel grinned. "I don't think he'd
appreciate that," she replied. "We'd
better leave it here, in case somebody
comes back for it."

Kirsty put the tractor down on a flat
patch of grass where it was easy to spot.
As she straightened up, she noticed some
strange-looking shiny stones. "Are those
rocks over there?" she asked.

Rachel turned and looked where her
friend was pointing. She saw a few big
brown objects under the
chestnut tree on one
side of the
meadow. "That's
funny," she said,
frowning. "I've
never noticed
those before. Let's
go and take a
closer look."

Kirsty and
Rachel ran over to

the tree. The things that Kirsty had
spotted were about the size and shape of
soccer balls. They were a glossy
chocolate brown color.
"Well, they're not
rocks," Kirsty
said, touching
one of them.
It felt cool
and smooth
under her
hand. "They
look more like . . . giant chestnuts!"

Rachel touched one, too. "They *do*
look like chestnuts," she agreed. "But
whoever heard of a chestnut this big?"

Before Kirsty could reply, Buttons
bounded over, barking excitedly.

Then he ran back to a patch of grass

a few feet away, sniffed it eagerly, and barked again.

Rachel went to see what he'd found. "Kirsty, quick!" she called, her eyes wide. "Come and look at these sheep!"

"Sheep?" echoed Kirsty, running over to join her friend. She couldn't see any sheep, but as she got closer to her friend she heard a tiny but clear *Ba-a-a-a!*

Rachel pointed down at the grass and Kirsty looked down, too.

"Tiny sheep!" Kirsty gasped in surprise. "Oh, wow! Are they real?"

Down by their feet was a flock of the tiniest sheep Kirsty and Rachel had ever seen. Sheep the size of mice! Chestnuts the size of soccer balls! What was going on?

Rachel's eyes were bright. "There is definitely magic in the air today," she breathed.

"There must be another magic jewel nearby," Kirsty added, feeling a thrill of excitement.

Quickly, the girls put the dogs on their leashes and tied them to the fence, so that the tiny sheep wouldn't accidentally get stepped on.

Just then, Rachel clutched Kirsty's arm. "Kirsty!" she squealed. "Look!"

Both girls stared. A large golden leaf was floating down from the chestnut tree in front of them. And there, sitting on top of it as if she was riding a magic carpet, was a tiny beaming fairy.

Seeing Red

"Wheeeeee!" squealed the fairy breathlessly. "Hello, girls!"

Kirsty and Rachel laughed as the golden leaf sailed down to the ground. The fairy jumped off and twirled up into the air, her wings beating so quickly they were a blur of glittering colors. She had wavy dark brown hair, and wore a

scarlet dress decorated with a pretty flower. She also wore little, glittery red shoes that twinkled in the sunlight.

"It's Scarlett the Garnet Fairy," Rachel cried, recognizing her right away. "Hello, Scarlett!"

"Of course!" Kirsty said, as she remembered something King Oberon had told them. "The garnet controls growing and shrinking magic!" she exclaimed. "That's why the chestnuts are so huge. . . ."

"And the sheep are so tiny," Rachel added with a smile.

"Exactly," Scarlett said. She waved her wand hopefully, but only a few red sparkles scattered from it. They fizzled and sputtered out in the grass. "And unfortunately, without the garnet, I don't have enough magic to turn things back to their proper sizes. We have to find the

garnet before it
changes anything
else."

She flew over to
perch on Kirsty's
shoulder. "India
told me that you
had a run-in with
Jack Frost's goblins
yesterday," she said,
shivering at the thought. "Let's try and
find the garnet before any goblins show
up today!"

"We'll start right away," Rachel said,
and Kirsty nodded.

"Great," Scarlett replied, smiling. "I'll
check the vegetable patch over there."

"And we'll search this field," Kirsty
said. "Come on, Rachel."

The girls walked slowly across the meadow, scanning the grass for any sign of the garnet. They were just passing a haystack when something very strange happened.

"My legs are tingling!" Kirsty gasped.

"We're shrinking!" Rachel cried as she saw the ground rushing toward her.

The girls had been fairy-size before, but then they'd always had pretty wings to fly with, too! Not this time. They had simply shrunk! Suddenly the haystack seemed like a mountain in front of them, and the grass was waist-high.

"The garnet must be very close, if the magic is working on us now," Kirsty pointed out.

"Scarlett! Hey, Scarlett!" Rachel shouted, trying to attract the fairy's attention. But her voice had shrunk, too. Scarlett couldn't hear her tiny call. "Rachel, look at the

top of the haystack," Kirsty cried, pointing upward. "It's glowing red!"

Rachel peered up at the haystack, and sure enough, something at the top was shining a deep red color. "It must be the garnet!" she declared. "Let's climb up and get it for Scarlett."

"Good idea," Kirsty agreed.

The two girls began to climb the
haystack. It was very hard work!
The hay was sharp and slippery, and it
was difficult to get a grip on the smooth
stalks. Little by little, the girls drew closer
to the magic garnet.

Just as Kirsty was about to reach the
top, the piece of hay that she was
holding on to suddenly swayed and bent.
Kirsty clutched at another stalk, but it
snapped in two! "Help!" she cried,
desperately trying to hang on. "I'm
falling!"

A Scary Surprise

"Here!" Rachel yelled, leaning down to reach Kirsty. "Grab my hand!"

Kirsty clung onto her friend's outstretched fingers, her heart pounding. "Thanks," she said shakily as her feet found a strong straw and Rachel helped pull her back up.

The girls climbed carefully up to the
top. Then Rachel gave a triumphant cry.
"We found it!" she cheered. In front of
them lay the glittering red garnet. The
sun shone through it, casting a rich, rosy
light across the hay.

"Wow!" breathed Kirsty. The jewel

seemed even more
impressive now
that the girls were
fairy-size. It was
no bigger than a
hen's egg, but
right now that
was almost as
tall as Rachel
and Kirsty!

"Scarlett!" both girls
shouted. They waved their arms around
at the top of the haystack, hoping the
fairy would see or hear them.

But Scarlett was still searching in the
vegetable patch. She had no idea that
her jewel had been found.

Then Kirsty had an idea. "What if we
turn the garnet around so that its red

light shines over to Scarlett?" she
suggested. "That will get her
attention."

"Perfect!" Rachel
agreed. "I bet it's
heavy, though. I
think we'll have
to lift it
together."

Kirsty took
hold of one side
of the jewel, and
Rachel held the
other. Then Kirsty
counted, "One . . . two . . .
three!" Together, the girls
turned the garnet so that its rosy
light was shining right at Scarlett.

The little fairy turned around. When

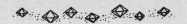

she saw the girls with the
garnet, her face lit up.
"Hooray!" she cried,
leaping into the air
and twirling for joy.
"You found it!"
Kirsty and Rachel
both took a hand off
the jewel to
wave at her.
When they did,
the garnet
slipped slightly.
Its sparkling red
light danced
farther down
the vegetable
patch, flickering over
a nearby scarecrow.

And then, to the girls' surprise, the scarecrow moved!

Rachel and Kirsty stared in amazement as the scarecrow jumped down from its wooden stand and started lumbering its way toward the haystack.

"What's happening?" Rachel asked. "Do you think it's more fairy magic?"

"I don't know," Kirsty replied. "I didn't think the garnet could do that." She watched the scarecrow walking jerkily toward them and suddenly felt nervous. "It's coming this way. What do you think it wants?"

Rachel narrowed her eyes and stared hard at the scarecrow. "Hang on a minute," she said. "Look at its green, pointy nose. That's not a scarecrow — it's a goblin!"

"Oh, no!" Kirsty cried, grabbing Rachel's arm in fright. "Look at how big it is!"

"It's as big as a grown-up," Rachel said anxiously, biting her lip. All of a sudden, she felt smaller than ever. How would she and Kirsty protect the garnet? They were so tiny, and the goblin was so huge! "Oh, hurry up, Scarlett! Come and get the garnet!" she yelled.

Scarlett was flying over as fast as she could, a determined look on her face. "I'm coming," she cried. "Hang on, girls!"

Kirsty gulped, still holding onto Rachel. "Look!" she said, pointing at the scarecrow.

It had stopped walking and was pulling off its long coat. And underneath the coat, there wasn't just one goblin, there were two. One was standing on the other's shoulders! The top goblin jumped down. As Rachel and Kirsty watched in horror, both goblins started running as fast as they could toward the garnet — and the girls.

Kidnapped!

"Let's get out of here," Kirsty cried. She
and Rachel began to clamber back down
the haystack as quickly as they could,
carrying the garnet between them.
The jewel felt strangely warm in their
hands.

"My fingers are tingling," Rachel called
out. "Do you think that means — ?"

But Rachel's words were cut off.
The garnet's magic was working
again — and this time, both girls were
growing. They clung tightly to
the jewel as their legs
lengthened, and their heads
moved up toward the sky.
Suddenly, the haystack,
which had seemed like
such a mountain to
climb, was nothing
more than a regular
haystack. It couldn't
hold the weight of the
two girls!
"I'm sinking," Rachel
panted as her feet sunk
into the hay. "We're too
heavy for the haystack now."

Scarlett arrived at that moment, looking anxious. "I'll try to use my magic to get you out of there!" she cried, waving her wand quickly. But only one glittering red sparkle fell out. It fizzled uselessly on the grass. "Oh, no, here come the goblins!" she cried, fluttering protectively in front of Kirsty and Rachel.

"Oh, dear! Oh, dear!" chuckled the taller goblin. He watched as the girls floundered around in the waist-deep hay.

The other, shorter goblin was close
behind. "I think we'll take that garnet,
thank you very much," he declared,
reaching out to snatch it from
Rachel's hand.

"Oh, no you don't!" Rachel cried,
throwing the precious stone into the air
before the goblin could grab it. "Catch,
Scarlett!"

Scarlett caught the garnet just in time but, in the human world, it was too big and heavy for her to fly with. She quickly sunk down through the air under the weight of the jewel, flapping her wings as hard as she could to keep from falling too far.

Kirsty could see that Scarlett was trying

to angle her wand so it would touch
the stone. The little fairy was trying
to recharge her wand with growing
and shrinking magic! But before she
could do that, poor Scarlett lost her
grip on the wand. It tumbled down
into the hay.

Luckily, Kirsty pounced
on the wand before
either of the
goblins could
reach it. Then
something
terrible
happened. The
shorter goblin whipped off his scarecrow
hat and held it out under the falling
fairy.

"Help!" Scarlett cried as she plunged helplessly into the dark hat.

"Gotcha!" cheered the goblin. "A garnet *and* a fairy — that's a bonus!"

"Hey!" called Rachel, kicking the hay in an attempt to get out of it. "Let Scarlett go, right now!"

"No way!" Both goblins laughed nastily — and ran away.

As the two girls finally scrambled out of the haystack, the goblins sprinted across the field with Scarlett and the garnet still trapped inside the scarecrow hat. Scarlett couldn't fly out because the goblin held the opening of the hat shut! Kirsty and Rachel could hear the goblins singing happily.

"Twinkle, twinkle, garnet stone,
You are never going home.
Jack Frost wants you hidden away.
Out of Fairyland you'll stay.
Sparkle, sparkle, on and on
The fairies' magic will soon be gone!"

"Come back!" shouted Kirsty angrily. "Rachel, we have to get that scarecrow hat . . . before it's too late!"

Dogs to the Rescue

As Rachel and Kirsty took off after the goblins, they looked around for anything that could help them rescue Scarlett. Then Kirsty's gaze fell on Cloud and Buttons. She remembered that, in the past, the goblins had been scared of dogs. "Wait!" she called to Rachel, thinking

fast. "Maybe Buttons and Cloud can help us!"

It seemed like the dogs had already had the same idea. They were both pulling on their leashes and barking at the goblins.

"Come on, boy," Rachel said, letting Buttons off his leash. "Let's go goblin catching!"

"You too, Cloud," Kirsty said, unclipping his leash. "Go, dogs, go!" Cloud and Buttons did not need to be told twice. With a loud chorus of barks, they both ran eagerly toward the goblins.

The goblin carrying the scarecrow hat looked back over his shoulder and screeched with fear when he saw the dogs. "Quick!" he yelled to his friend. "Climb on top of the scarecrow stand!"

Both goblins scrambled back up the wooden stand. They clung tightly to its beams.

Woof! Woof! Woof! Buttons and Cloud barked happily, jumping up and trying to lick the goblins' toes.

"Eek!" yelped the tall goblin, pulling his feet up. "Go away, you horrible mutts!"

Kirsty and Rachel ran over. "This is all your fault," they heard the tall goblin hiss at his friend. "It was your idea to climb up here!"

"Well, if you ran faster we could have been out of here by now," the short one moaned back.

"Is everything OK?" Kirsty asked sweetly. She patted Cloud and Buttons, who were still looking up hopefully at the goblins. They wanted to play!

"No!" snapped the tall goblin.

"Just send the dogs away!" the short goblin begged.

"I don't think so," Rachel replied cheerfully. "Unless . . ."

"What? What?" the goblins cried together.

"Unless you set Scarlett free," Kirsty finished.

The short goblin looked thoughtful and scratched his leathery green head. "All right," he said at last. "The fairy can go. But the garnet is staying right here, in my hat."

"OK," the girls agreed.

Rachel grabbed both dogs by their collars and held them back. "Now, let Scarlett go," she said.

The goblin carefully opened the

hat just wide enough for Scarlett to
flutter out.

She zoomed through the gap and flew
over to land on Kirsty's shoulder. "Thank
you," she said as Kirsty
handed her wand back.
"That hat smelled
awful!"

"Well, you're still not
getting your hands on
our jewel," the goblin said,
reaching into the hat to pat the garnet.
"You might as well — hey!" he suddenly
yelped in surprise. "What's happening?"

Kirsty, Rachel, and Scarlett stared at
the goblin. And then all three of them
began to laugh.

"It's the garnet!" Scarlett laughed. "It's
making him shrink!"

Sure enough, the short goblin was growing even shorter before their eyes. "Help! Make it stop!" he squeaked in a tiny voice.

His friend was chuckling loudly — but not for long. Now that there was one big goblin and one tiny goblin on the scarecrow's stand, the whole thing was off balance.

"*Whoa!*" the big goblin cried as he began to fall. "Help!"

Goblins on the Run

Splat!

The girls backed out of the way just as the large goblin landed on the ground. "Oof!" he panted. "Stupid garnet!"

Woof! barked the dogs, running over and licking the goblin playfully. *Woof! Woof!*

Rachel and Kirsty couldn't help smiling

as the goblin rolled around, helpless with laughter. "It tickles!" he roared. "Ooh, it tickles!"

Then Kirsty remembered the garnet. She rushed over to the scarecrow pole where the tiny goblin was still hanging on. Kirsty plucked the hat easily from his arms.

"Hooray!" cheered Scarlett when she saw the magic garnet gleaming in Kirsty's hand. "Great job, Kirsty!"

"We did it!" Rachel cried. "We found another jewel."

The girls and Scarlett headed back toward the farmhouse. They called the dogs to follow them, once they were a safe distance from the goblins.

Then Scarlett carefully touched her wand to the magic garnet and waved it in the air. A stream of glittering red fairy dust flooded out across the fields. A smile lit up Scarlett's face. "That's more like it!" she said.

Baa! Baa! The sheep were suddenly back to their normal size. Cloud and Buttons stared at them in confusion, wondering where they had come from.

Cloud sniffed at a stray red sparkle and jumped as it fizzed into thin air under his nose.

Kirsty turned to look at the chestnut tree. The giant chestnuts had disappeared. They had shrunk to their normal size again! And what was that, in the middle of the field?

"Mr. Johnson's tractor!" Rachel laughed. "The garnet must have shrunk that, too. Remember, we thought it was a toy?"

Kirsty grinned as the last few bright twinkles of fairy magic disappeared from

the tractor's wheels. "Now Mr. Johnson will be in a good mood again," she said happily.

"And so will King Oberon and Queen Titania when I send this garnet back to Fairyland," Scarlett added.

The tiny goblin had been turned back to his regular size, too. The girls and Scarlett watched as he jumped down from the wooden stand and stomped away with his goblin friend. Although the girls couldn't hear what they were saying, it was clear that they were arguing again.

Scarlett chuckled. "And that's the last

we'll see of them," she said,
sounding satisfied. She
touched her wand to the
garnet once more and it
vanished in a fountain of
glittering red fairy dust.

"Now the garnet is
safely back in Fairyland,"
Rachel said with a sigh of
relief. The air where the garnet had been
shimmered for a second, then returned to
normal.

"And I should be going back, too,"
Scarlett added, hugging the girls good-
bye. "Thank you for all your help, Kirsty
and Rachel. And good luck finding the
other magic jewels!"

The girls waved as the tiny fairy
zoomed away to Fairyland.

"Phew," Rachel said as they headed
back to the farmhouse. "That was close.
For a minute, I thought the goblins were
going to get away with the garnet *and*
Scarlett."

Kirsty ruffled Cloud's shaggy coat.
"Well, thanks to these two
dogs, both Scarlett and the
garnet are safe and
sound," she declared
with a smile.

Rachel grinned at
Kirsty. "Come on," she
said, breaking into a run.
"We'll have more fairy adventures soon,
but for now, I'm starving. I wonder if Mrs.
Johnson has any more of those plums left."

"I hope so," Kirsty said, running after
her friend. "Race you there!"

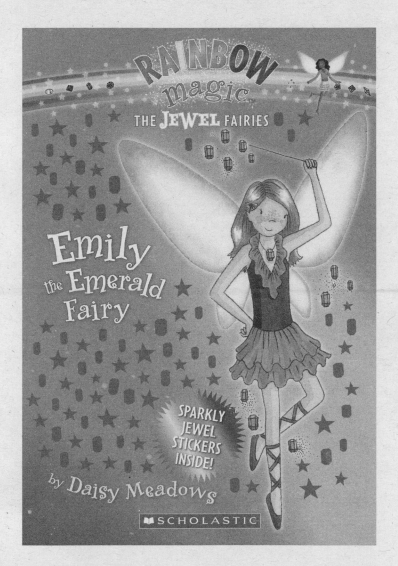

RAINBOW magic

THE JEWEL FAIRIES

Emily the Emerald Fairy

SPARKLY JEWEL STICKERS INSIDE!

by Daisy Meadows

SCHOLASTIC

To Annabelle Argent — with love
and fairy magic

Special thanks to
Narinder Dhami

Toy Trouble

"Wow!" Kirsty Tate gasped, her eyes wide with amazement. "This is the biggest toy store I've ever seen!"

Her best friend, Rachel Walker, laughed. "I know," she agreed. "Isn't it great?"

Kirsty nodded. Wherever she turned,

there was something wonderful to see. In
one corner of the store was a huge display
of dolls in every shape and size, along
with an amazing number of dollhouses.
A special roped-off area was filled with
remote-control cars, buses, trucks, and
airplanes. Nearby stood rows of bikes,
skateboards, and scooters.

Shelves were piled high with every
board game Kirsty could think of, plus

stacks of cool computer games. Colorful
kites hung from the ceiling, along with
big balloons and spinning mobiles. Kirsty
had never seen anything like it, and this
was only the first floor!

"Look over there, Kirsty," Rachel said,
pointing at the dolls.

Kirsty saw a sign that read MEET FAIRY
FLORENCE AND HER FRIENDS. She stared
at the dolls displayed around the sign.

Fairy Florence wore a long pink dress. She looked boring and old-fashioned. Kirsty and Rachel glanced at each other and burst out laughing.

"Fairy Florence doesn't look like a real fairy at all!" Rachel whispered, and Kirsty nodded.

Rachel and Kirsty knew what real

fairies looked like because they'd met
them . . . many times! The two girls had
often visited Fairyland to help their fairy
friends when they were in trouble. The
problems were usually caused by icy Jack
Frost. He was always making trouble
with the help of his mean goblins.

Just a few days earlier, King Oberon
and Queen Titania had asked Rachel and
Kirsty to help them. Jack Frost had stolen
the seven magic jewels from the queen's
crown. The jewels were very important,
because they controlled a lot of the
magic in Fairyland.

Jack Frost had wanted the magic for
himself, but after the heat and light of the
jewels began to melt his ice castle, he had
angrily thrown the gems far into the

human world. Now it was up to the girls
to return the jewels to Fairyland, before
the fairies' magic ran out for good.

"I hope we can find the rest of the
magic jewels before I go home," Kirsty
said to Rachel, looking worried. "After
all, I'm only staying with you until the
end of school break."

"Well, we found India's moonstone and
Scarlett's garnet," Rachel reminded her.

"We just have to keep our eyes open
for the others."

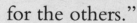

"Yes, we have to
watch out for goblins
and magic jewels!"
Kirsty said. The girls
knew that Jack Frost
had sent his goblins to

find and guard the gems, so that the fairies wouldn't get them back.

"Here you are, girls," said Rachel's dad as he joined them. "Do you two want to look around the toy store on your own? We can meet up in a little while."

"Dad can't wait to check out the train section," Rachel told Kirsty with a grin. "It's his favorite part of the store."

Mr. Walker laughed. "Ah, but today I have the perfect excuse," he said. "I'm buying something for my godson, Mark.

It's his birthday soon, and he loves trains."

Toot, toot!

The sudden sound of a whistle made Kirsty jump.

"Watch out, Kirsty!" Rachel cried with a smile. "There's a train coming!"

Kirsty looked up. For the first time, she noticed that a train track ran around 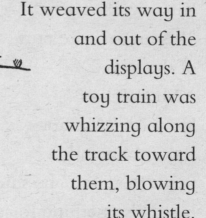 the store above their heads. It weaved its way in and out of the displays. A toy train was whizzing along the track toward them, blowing its whistle.

"Isn't it fun?" Mr.

Walker asked, beaming as the train sped by. "I'll see you two later. Meet me at the front entrance in half an hour."

"OK," Rachel replied. She grinned at Kirsty. "Come on, let's take a look around."

The girls wandered past the dolls, and over to a roped-off area where customers were playing with remote-control cars.

"Aren't they fast?" Kirsty remarked, staring at a bright red car that was zooming back and forth across the floor.

"I think we should buy this red one," the woman next to Kirsty said,

turning to her husband with a smile. "Stuart will love it!"

Her husband, who held the controls in his hand, pushed a button. The car skidded to a stop, then flipped over and landed on its wheels before zooming off again.

"That's cool!" Kirsty gasped, very impressed.

"Isn't it?" the woman agreed, giving the two girls a friendly smile. "Our little boy, Stuart, will really enjoy playing with it." She glanced at her husband, who was now making the car whiz around in circles. "If he gets a chance, that is!"

Rachel and Kirsty laughed. They were just about to walk away when, suddenly, Kirsty caught sight of something out of the corner of her eye. Something silvery and glittering . . .

Kirsty spun around. There was a tall
mirror on the wall near her, and the
surface of the glass was moving. It
rippled and shimmered, just like a pool of
water.

"Oh!" Kirsty gasped.
"Rachel, look!"

Rachel stared at the
shimmering surface of
the mirror, and her eyes
widened. "Is it
magic?" she
whispered.

As the girls
watched in
amazement, a
reflection appeared
in the glass. Rachel
and Kirsty could see

a small boy, about seven years old, playing with the same shiny red car from the store. The boy pushed a button on the remote control, smiling as he watched the toy. The little red car came whizzing straight toward the girls!

Rachel and Kirsty turned around quickly, ready to jump out of the way of the speeding car. But to their amazement, there was nothing there. The boy and his toy car had disappeared!

Mirror Magic

Both Kirsty and Rachel blinked hard and looked around the store. There were little boys nearby, but they didn't see the boy they had been watching in the mirror. How could he have disappeared so quickly?

"What just happened?" Rachel asked,

rubbing her eyes. "Were we seeing things?"

Kirsty turned back to the mirror again. The magical shimmer was gone now, and the glass looked completely flat and normal again. In the mirror, Kirsty saw the reflection of the man and woman who had been looking at the red car. Now they were paying for the toy at the counter behind her.

"But the boy looked so real," she said to Rachel.

"It must be fairy magic," Rachel whispered as they walked away. "But what does it mean?"

"I don't know," Kirsty replied. "Maybe we'll find out soon!"

The girls walked into another part of the store that was full of practical jokes and little toys. There were shelves full of rubber spiders, plastic soldiers, dinosaurs, farm animals, pencils, erasers, paints, and beads.

"Mom!" A little girl ran down the aisle toward Rachel and Kirsty. She looked very excited, and was waving a large, plastic bottle of bubble mixture in her hand. "Mom, where are you? I want this one! It says it blows the biggest bubbles in the whole world!"

But as the little girl passed Rachel and Kirsty, the bottle slipped from her fingers. It crashed to the floor and cracked open. Frothy bubble mix spilled out.

"Oh!" the little girl gasped, and burst into tears.

"It's OK, don't cry," Kirsty said quickly. "It was an accident."

Just then, the little girl's mom hurried toward them, followed by a salesperson.

"Oh, Katie!" the woman said, giving her daughter a hug. "Don't worry, I'll buy you another one."

"And we'll get that cleaned up right away," said the salesclerk kindly.

"Thank you so much," Katie's mom said gratefully.

Smiling now, the little girl and her mom walked off to find another bottle of bubbles, while the salesperson went to get a mop.

"Should we go look at the dollhouses?" Kirsty suggested.

But Rachel was staring at the floor in amazement. "Kirsty, look at that!" she whispered, clutching her friend's arm.

Kirsty looked down. The pool of bubble mixture was shimmering and

rippling on the floor, just like the mirror! Slowly, the girls saw a picture form in the liquid. It was Katie. She seemed to be playing happily in a sunny garden, blowing big, beautiful bubbles.

"This *has* to be fairy magic," Rachel said as the picture faded. "I think we're seeing things that are going to happen in the future! We saw Katie playing with her bubbles at home, and the little boy with the red car must have been Stuart."

Kirsty looked thoughtful. "Do you think the magic emerald could be nearby?" she asked. "That's the jewel that controls seeing magic."

Rachel nodded. "I think you're right —" she began.

Toot, toot!

The girls glanced up to see the store's little train chugging along its track, just above their heads.

But as it came closer, Rachel stared.

"There's something sparkly in the first car of the train," she pointed out.

Kirsty peered hard at the train and suddenly realized what Rachel had seen. "It's Emily the Emerald Fairy!" she gasped happily.

A Goblin Drops By

Emily was leaning out of the train and waving her sparkly, emerald-green wand at Rachel and Kirsty. As the train came closer to the girls, Emily fluttered out and landed on Rachel's shoulder. She wore a short green dress and ballet slippers in exactly the same color. Long, shiny red hair tumbled down her back. It was held

away from her face by a dazzling
emerald clip in the shape of a dragonfly.

"At last!" Emily beamed, her green
eyes sparkling. "I'm so happy to see you.
I've been looking for you everywhere!"

"And we're happy to see you," Kirsty
replied. "Some really strange things have
been happening around here."

"Let's go over behind that display

rack," said Rachel quickly, looking around to make sure that nobody was watching them. "We have lots to tell you, Emily!"

When they were safely hidden from the other customers, the girls told Emily about the pictures they'd seen in the mirror and the bubble mixture.

Emily nodded.

"That's seeing magic," she told them. "It means my emerald is nearby."

"We'll help you look for it," said Kirsty.

"But there are lots of places it could

be," Rachel added, frowning as she looked around the enormous store.

"And there are lots of places for goblins to hide, too," Emily pointed out. She fluttered down and slipped into Rachel's pocket. "We need to be careful."

The two girls walked into the middle of the store and began to wander through the aisles. Emily peeked out of Rachel's pocket.

Suddenly Rachel grabbed Kirsty's arm. "What's that green sparkle over there?" she asked excitedly.

"Where?" Kirsty asked.

"In the doll section," Rachel replied, pointing. Her heart pounding, she led the way across the room to the glimmer of green she had seen. "I know it's around here somewhere."

"Was that it?" Kirsty asked, pointing at one of the dolls. It was wearing a necklace of shiny green beads that glittered in the light.

Rachel looked at the doll more closely, and her face fell. "Yes, I think it was," she said, sighing.

"Don't worry," said Emily, popping her head out of Rachel's pocket. "I'm sure we'll find it if we keep looking."

The girls walked around the store, searching through the toys. They still didn't see any sign of the magic emerald.

"There's a green glow over there!" Emily said suddenly. "What is it?"

The girls rushed over to take a look.

But they were disappointed to find that the green light was coming from a computer game. "I really don't think the emerald is anywhere down here," said Rachel, shaking her head.

Kirsty glanced upward. "What about the next floor up?" she suggested.

The girls and Emily took the elevator up to the next floor. It was much quieter there. There were hardly any customers around, and the only salesclerk in sight was busy with some paperwork behind the counter.

"My emerald must be here somewhere," Emily whispered as the girls walked out of the elevator. "It's not far away. I can feel it!"

Kirsty blinked. Was that a green sparkle she'd just spotted, or was she imagining things? No, there it was again. "I see something!" she said excitedly. "Over there, in the stuffed animal section."

The girls and Emily hurried over to take a closer look. There were hundreds of stuffed animals. Rachel and Kirsty gazed around at the cuddly cats, dogs,

cows, penguins, zebras, and other
creatures. There was even a big golden
lion, with a shaggy bronze mane.

"Look," Kirsty said, pointing at a furry
black cat. It sat at the very top of a pile
of stuffed animals, and it had long, silky
fur. But Rachel saw that it also had
almond-shaped green eyes that glittered
in the light.

"Could one of the cat's eyes be your

emerald, Emily?" asked Rachel, looking
up at the toy.

"Let me see," Emily replied. She
fluttered out of Rachel's pocket and flew
up to the cat, looking closely at its eyes.
After a moment, she let out a tiny squeal
of delight, and pointed to the cat's right
eye. "This is my
emerald!" she
cried.

Kirsty and
Rachel beamed
at each other.

"Kirsty, could
you get the cat
down, please?"
Emily called. "It's
too heavy for me to
pick up."

Kirsty nodded and stretched up toward the cat. If she stood on her tiptoes, she thought she would just be able to reach it.

Vrrrroooom!

Kirsty glanced up when she heard the growl of an engine overhead. As she did, she saw that Rachel and Emily were also trying to figure out where the noise was coming from.

Suddenly, the girls spotted a large silver toy plane flying straight toward them.

The pilot wore flying goggles, gloves, and a long, white scarf. But Kirsty saw that his skin was green. One of Jack Frost's goblins was flying the plane!

Kirsty turned back to the magic

emerald, determined to grab it before the goblin arrived. But, just as she stretched out her hand for the toy cat, the plane swooped toward her. As it zoomed past, the goblin reached out with a gloved hand and snatched the cat right out of Kirsty's fingers!

Goblin Getaway

"Ha, ha, ha!" the goblin cackled gleefully. "The magic emerald is mine!"

"Come back!" Emily shouted as Kirsty and Rachel glanced at each other in dismay. "Give me my emerald!"

The goblin stuck his tongue out at her. "You can't catch me!" he sneered, and

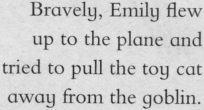

bent over the controls. The plane began
to turn.

"He's getting away!" Rachel gasped.

Bravely, Emily flew
up to the plane and
tried to pull the toy cat
away from the goblin.
He quickly let go of
the plane's controls
and gave her a shove.
The plane dipped
and swerved but the
goblin soon regained
control. Poor Emily
tumbled through the
air. Her wings flapped
wildly as she tried to recover her
balance. Luckily, she landed gently on the
pile of stuffed animals below.

Rachel turned to Kirsty. "Quick!" she cried. "You go make sure Emily is OK, and I'll try to stop the goblin from getting away."

Kirsty nodded. "Emily!" she called as she rushed to help the little fairy. "Are you all right?"

"I'm fine!" Emily panted, struggling to stand on the trunk of a cuddly pink elephant. "But please don't let that goblin escape with my emerald!"

Rachel looked around desperately for a way to stop the goblin in his tracks. His plane was heading toward the elevator and if he made it inside, Rachel thought they might never get the emerald back.

Suddenly, she spotted a huge bunch of helium balloons tied to one of the displays in the goblin's path. She raced over and untied the knot as quickly as she could. Just as the goblin flew overhead, Rachel let go of the balloons. They immediately soared upward, surrounding the plane on all sides.

"Hey, what's going on?" Rachel heard the goblin splutter. "I can't see anything!"

Rachel looked up. The goblin was trying to swat the balloons away, but to do that he had to let go of the controls. The plane dipped forward and nose-dived. "Help!" the goblin roared. He dropped the stuffed cat and covered his eyes with both hands. "I'm going to crash!"

The plane and the black cat both crash-landed in a pile of teddy bears and disappeared. Rachel, Kirsty, and Emily rushed over. Just then, the goblin began to climb out of the heap of toys, muttering under his breath.

"He dropped the emerald," Emily whispered to the girls. "Let's find it and get out of here."

Kirsty and Rachel began searching through the pile of stuffed animals. The

goblin glared at them and dived back into the heap of toys himself. He threw stuffed animals here and there as he burrowed out of sight.

"We have to find the emerald before he does," Kirsty said.

"Too late!" the goblin declared, as he crawled out from the bottom of the pile of toys. "You won't catch me now — and you won't get this back, either!" Then he waved the stuffed cat with the emerald eye at the girls, stuck out his tongue, and ran away.

Catch That Goblin!

"Catch him!" Emily cried. "He still has my emerald!"

Rachel and Kirsty ran after the goblin, with Emily flying alongside them. Luckily, there weren't any other customers around to see the chase. But the goblin was very tricky. He dodged back and forth, disappearing behind displays. He always managed to stay one step ahead of the girls.

Kirsty slowed down and looked around.

"Where did he go now?" she asked. The goblin was nowhere to be seen.

"He was here a minute ago," Rachel said, confused. "He couldn't have just disappeared."

"There he is!" Emily shouted, pointing with her sparkly wand.

The girls turned and saw the goblin
running toward the stairs as fast as he
could. The toy cat
bobbed up and
down in his arms.

"Don't let him
get away!"
Rachel gasped,
sprinting after
the goblin.

The sudden
sound of footsteps
coming up the
stairs made the
goblin skid to a
stop. Realizing
that the stairs were
blocked, he frantically looked around for
another way to escape. Then he ducked

behind some shelves stacked with toy cars and trucks.

The girls and Emily followed. They raced down one aisle just in time to see the goblin turn the corner into the next.

"I think we're catching up," said Kirsty. "Keep going!"

Rachel and Kirsty dashed around the
corner and almost
tripped.

The goblin was
pulling boxes of
toys off the shelves
and throwing them
in the girls' path!

"Wait a minute,
girls!" Emily called as
the goblin ran off
again, cackling with glee.
With an expert wave of her wand, Emily
scattered fairy dust over the boxes.
Immediately, they floated up into the air
and neatly stacked themselves back on
the shelves.

"Why don't we split up?" Rachel

whispered to Kirsty and Emily. "Then maybe we can trap him."

"Good idea," Kirsty agreed.

At the end of the aisle, Kirsty and Emily went left, and Rachel went right. The goblin had disappeared again. But as Rachel ran between the shelves of toys, she saw him dash across the aisle, right in front of her.

"Got you!" she panted, reaching out to grab him by the shoulder.

But the goblin was too quick for her. He snatched a blue skateboard from a nearby shelf, flung it to the floor, and jumped on. Rachel's fingers clutched at thin air as the goblin rolled across the polished floor.

"You almost had him, Rachel!" Emily shouted, flying over to her.

"Look!" Kirsty gasped, rushing to join her friends. "He's heading for the elevator!"

The elevator doors stood open, waiting for passengers to enter. The skateboard was zooming right toward them! The goblin glanced back at the girls with a smug smile, waving the toy cat triumphantly.

"Oh, no, we'll never catch him now!" wailed Emily.

But Kirsty wasn't going to give up yet. She looked at the toys on the shelves around her, searching for something, anything, that might stop the goblin. Her gaze fell on a stack of brightly painted boomerangs. "Emily, can you use your magic to help me?" she asked, grabbing one from the top of the pile.

Emily nodded and lifted her wand. Kirsty aimed the boomerang at the toy cat in the goblin's hand, and threw it. The boomerang whistled through the air, but as it got closer to the goblin, it started to drift off course. Rachel bit her lip. It looked like the goblin was going to get away with the emerald after

all, no matter how hard they tried to stop him!

But Emily waved her wand, and a cloud of sparkling fairy dust shot after the boomerang. As soon as the fairy magic touched the toy, the boomerang swerved back on course. It flew straight toward the goblin like an arrow.

The friends watched as the boomerang spun through the air and knocked the toy cat right out of the goblin's hand!

The cat fell to the floor, but the skateboard kept going. The goblin let out a howl. He had lost the magic emerald!

Going Up

"Pesky fairy magic!" the goblin shouted.
But there was nothing he could do. The
skateboard was zooming along too fast
for him to jump off. He glanced over his
shoulder just as Kirsty and Rachel ran
forward and picked up the toy cat.

"Give that back!" yelled the goblin as

the skateboard headed toward the elevator. "You must be joking!" Rachel laughed. "Shouldn't you watch where you're going?" called Kirsty. The skateboard whizzed through the open doors of the elevator and crashed into the back wall. The goblin fell on the floor in a heap. He staggered to his feet, unhurt, but he looked very angry. He made a rush for the elevator doors, but they slammed shut. He was trapped inside. *Ting!* The elevator began to move upward.

"Good-bye, goblin!" Emily called.

Kirsty and Rachel laughed, and they could hear a muffled roar of rage from inside the elevator.

"Girls, you've done it again," Emily cried, fluttering down to sit on Kirsty's shoulder. "How can I ever thank you?"

"We're just glad we got your emerald back," replied Kirsty, holding up the stuffed black cat. The beautiful magic emerald winked and sparkled at them.

"Sorry, kitty," Emily said, smiling at the toy cat, "but I need my emerald more than you do!" She raised her wand and a shower of green sparkles floated down over the black cat. The magic emerald fell gently into Kirsty's hand, and a new green eye appeared in its place.

"And now it's back to Fairyland for you," Emily added, touching her wand to the jewel. "Queen Titania and King Oberon will be very happy to see you!"

A fountain of sparkling green fairy dust shot up from the

jewel. The emerald
vanished from
Kirsty's hand.

"Rachel, we'd
better go down and
meet your dad,"
Kirsty said, looking at
her watch.

"I think we'll use the stairs!" Rachel
agreed, laughing.

"Thank you for your help, girls," Emily
said in her pretty voice.
"Every jewel you find
brings us one step closer
to returning the jewels'
magic to Fairyland." She
waved her wand. "Good-
bye, and good luck!" Then
she disappeared in a flash
of fairy dust.

Rachel and Kirsty grinned at each other and hurried downstairs.

Rachel's dad was waiting by the store's main entrance, carrying lots of shopping bags. "Ah, there you are, girls," he said with a grin. "Will you give me a hand with these?" He handed each of them a bag.

"Lucky Mark!" said Rachel, taking a peek inside. "He's going to get lots of presents for his birthday."

Her dad looked embarrassed. "Well, some of these things are for me, actually," he said. "I'm thinking of putting a toy train track in the attic."

Rachel laughed. "That sounds like a great idea, Dad."

"That was quite an adventure!" Kirsty

whispered to Rachel as they followed
Mr. Walker out of the store.

Rachel nodded. Then she grinned and
gestured toward her dad, who was
marching happily down the street with
his bags, eagerly explaining
his plans for the train
track in the attic.
"From the sound
of it, our next
adventure is going
to involve trains,
not fairies!" she said,
laughing. Somehow,
both girls knew that
wasn't true. They'd surely see their fairy
friends again soon!

RAINBOW
magic
THE JEWEL FAIRIES

Chloe
the Topaz
Fairy

by Daisy Meadows

SPARKLY
JEWEL
STICKERS
INSIDE!

SCHOLASTIC

To Rachel and Anna Prockter,
two fairy friends

Special thanks to

Linda Chapman

Goblins in Disguise

"There's a cool costume store!" Kirsty Tate said, pointing at one of the shops on Cherrywell's busy main street.

"Fun!" Rachel Walker replied happily. "Let's go pick out costumes for Isabel's Halloween party before the bus comes."

"OK," Kirsty agreed. She was staying at Rachel's house for the week, and the

girls had just gone bowling with some
of Rachel's friends from school. One of
them, Isabel, had invited everyone to a
Halloween party over the weekend.

"What do
you want to
dress up as?"
Kirsty asked
Rachel.
"Something
magical, of
course!"
Rachel replied
with a grin.
Kirsty smiled
back. She and Rachel
loved magic. It was because they shared
an amazing secret: They were friends
with the fairies!

Their magical adventures had all started one summer. The girls had helped the fairies stop mean Jack Frost from taking the color out of Fairyland. Since then, the Fairy King and Queen had asked for their help again and again. In fact, Rachel and Kirsty were right in the middle of another fairy adventure. Jack Frost was still causing trouble!

This time, he'd stolen seven sparkling jewels from Queen Titania's crown. The jewels were very special because they controlled important fairy powers, like the ability to fly, or to give children in the human world sweet dreams. Every year, in a special celebration, the fairies recharged their wands with the jewels' magic. This year's ceremony was just around the corner. If the jewels weren't

found by then, the fairies would run out of their special magic completely!

Jack Frost had hoped to keep the magic jewels for himself. But when their magic had started to melt his ice castle, he had gotten very angry. He cast a spell to throw the gems far into the human world. Then he sent his mean goblins to guard them, so the fairies couldn't get them back.

Rachel and Kirsty had already helped three of the Jewel Fairies track down their magic gems. But there were still four jewels left to find!

"Do you think we'll find another jewel today?" Rachel whispered as she and Kirsty ran up to the store.

"I hope so," Kirsty replied.

A small boy and his mom were looking

at the display in the store window.
There were colorful lanterns and two
mannequins wearing Halloween costumes.
One was dressed as a witch, and the
other as a goblin.

Suddenly, the boy gasped. "Mom! Did
you see that?" he cried. "That goblin
costume just moved!"

Rachel and Kirsty stopped and glanced
at each other.

"Don't be silly, Tom." The boy's mom laughed, leading him away. "It's time to go!"

"A goblin mannequin that moves?" Kirsty hissed to Rachel. "We'd better take a look."

The girls peered closely at the window display. The mannequin the boy had pointed out was wearing a green goblin costume and a little red hat. Rachel's eyes widened as she took in the goblin's beady eyes, long nose, and great big feet.

"That's not a goblin costume!" she exclaimed. "It's a *real* goblin!"

"And look at the witch," Kirsty added. The witch mannequin wore a long black skirt and a pointed hat, and held a broomstick. Its lumpy green nose and warty chin looked awfully goblinlike, though.

"The witch is a goblin, too!" Rachel gasped.

Kirsty grabbed Rachel's arm. "Oh, Rachel, if there are goblins in the window, maybe one of the fairies' magic jewels is inside the store!"

Looking Out for Magic

"Let's go take a look!" Rachel cried. The girls pushed the door open and hurried down three stone steps into the store. A salesperson came rushing over to meet them. She had curly brown hair and a cheerful smile. "Hello," she said, stepping around a large pile of pumpkin buckets near the door. "May I help you?"

Rachel could feel her heart pounding. "Um . . ." she began uncertainly. It was hard to concentrate, knowing that two goblins were standing just a few feet away.

"Could we look at some costumes, please?" Kirsty asked quickly. "We're going to a Halloween party over the weekend, and we don't have anything to wear."

The salesperson smiled. "Well, you've come to the right place! My name's Maggie. I'm sure I can find something for the two of you. What did you have in mind?"

Kirsty looked around and spotted a display of cat costumes. "I think I'd like to try a cat costume, please," she said.

"Well, we have lots of choices," Maggie replied. She turned to Rachel. "How about you, my dear?"

Rachel thought fast. They needed to search the store for the magic jewel. If Kirsty could keep Maggie busy, then maybe Rachel could look around. "I haven't quite decided yet," she replied truthfully. "Would it be OK if I look around a little bit?"

"Of course," Maggie answered. She smiled at Kirsty. "Now, why don't you come with me to the dressing room, and I'll find a cat costume in your size?"

As Kirsty headed off with Maggie,

Rachel glanced around the store. There were racks of costumes, and shelves piled high with wigs, makeup, and masks. Rachel noticed a container full of plastic swords and a stand packed with fairy wings and wands. *If there is a magic jewel in this store,* she thought, *it could be anywhere!*

Her eyes fell on a pirate display near

the back of the store. There were two mannequins dressed in pirate costumes.

They stood on a fake desert island, and each pirate had an eye patch. Between them was a palm tree and a huge treasure chest with gold chains and strings of pearls spilling from it. *That would be the perfect place to hide a jewel,* Rachel thought.

As she drew closer to the treasure chest, her heart seemed to skip a beat. The chest was glowing with a deep golden light. *Magic!* Rachel thought, looking at the way the gold chains glittered and gleamed. *It has to be!* Holding her breath, she lifted the heavy lid of the chest.

Suddenly, a fountain of orange-and-gold sparkles shot into the air. Rachel gasped and nearly dropped the lid. Twirling in the middle of the sparkles was a tiny fairy!

Costumes Galore!

"Hello!" called the fairy brightly. She was wearing a frilly yellow skirt, an orange wraparound top, and sparkling orange shoes. Her wavy black hair was held back by a red headband.

"Hi!" Rachel replied in delight. She thought she recognized the fairy. "Aren't you Chloe the Topaz Fairy?"

223

Chloe nodded. "Yes, I am."

Rachel glanced back over her shoulder. Luckily, Maggie was busy handing clothes to Kirsty. She hadn't noticed the fairy. Rachel led Chloe behind a costume rack. "Is your topaz in this store?" she asked. "Kirsty and I thought it seemed like a magic jewel was nearby."

"The magic topaz is definitely in here. I can feel it," Chloe responded, perching on Rachel's hand. "But I haven't been able to find it. I was searching through the treasure chest when the lid shut. I was trapped inside! Thanks for rescuing me."

"No problem," Rachel said with a smile. She peeked around the side of the costume rack. "Have you seen the goblins?"

Chloe looked alarmed. "Goblins! What goblins?"

"There are two goblins in the window display. They're pretending to be mannequins," Rachel explained.

Chloe shivered. "They must be here to guard the topaz. We'll have to try to send it back to Fairyland without the goblins noticing."

"Yes," Rachel agreed. "But we need to find it first. Where should we look?" Just then, she heard the dressing room door open. She peeked around the clothing rack to see how Kirsty was doing. "The cat costume fits you just fine," Maggie was saying to Kirsty. "But you need some cat ears! Wait there, and I'll get you some from the stockroom."

When Maggie walked away, Rachel hurried over to her friend. "Kirsty!" she hissed.

"What is it?" Kirsty asked eagerly. "Did you find something? Oh!" She gasped when she saw Chloe fluttering beside Rachel.

The little fairy grinned. "Hi, I'm Chloe," she said.

"Chloe's topaz is somewhere in this store," Rachel told Kirsty quietly. "We have to find it!"

"What does it look like?" Kirsty asked.

"It's a deep golden color," Chloe replied. "And it controls changing magic, so keep your eyes open for any strange changes."

"It might be hidden with those fairy wands," Rachel suggested, pointing to a display near by. "Let's check there."

"You do that, and I'll check the queen costume," Kirsty said, pointing to an outfit near the

window. It was a beautiful jeweled dress and cape with a crown of glittering gems. "The topaz could easily hide there." Just then, Rachel's sharp ears caught the sound of footsteps.

"Maggie's coming back!" she warned.
She and Chloe slipped behind the
costume rack again.

"Let's check the fairy wand display,"
Rachel whispered to Chloe. "If you hide
in the pocket of my coat, Maggie won't
be able to see you."

Chloe dived into Rachel's pocket, and
they headed over to look at the wands.

Meanwhile, Maggie handed Kirsty a pair of cat ears.

"Um," Kirsty began. "I'm really sorry, but I just noticed that queen costume. It's so beautiful! Would you mind if I tried that one on, instead?"

"Of course not!" Maggie replied cheerfully. "I'll go get it for you." She bustled over to the store window and took the costume off the mannequin. "Here we are!" she said, heading back to Kirsty with the costume in her arms.

As Maggie carried the costume past the

window, Kirsty heard a faint *pop*. The air behind Maggie shimmered with a golden glow. Then, to Kirsty's amazement, the witch costume on the goblin in the window changed into a suit of armor! Kirsty gasped and looked around quickly for her friends. She was sure that the costume change was the work of Chloe's magic topaz!

Lots of Changes

Maggie walked closer to Kirsty. Behind
her, the goblins in the window looked
around in confusion. The metal visor on
the suit of armor fell down with a dull
clunk, and the goblin inside let out a
muffled shriek of surprise.

Hearing the noise, Maggie turned
around. She stared at the suit of armor.

"Where did that come from?" she
murmured. "I thought there was a witch
costume in the window." She turned
back to Kirsty. "Did you see a witch
costume?"

Kirsty didn't know what to say. "Um, I
can't really remember," she replied.

"Maybe someone changed the
costumes yesterday. That was my day
off," Maggie explained. "But I'm
surprised I didn't notice earlier!"

Behind Maggie, Kirsty could see the
goblin in the red hat smirking at his
friend, who was
struggling to yank open
the heavy visor of his
helmet.

Meanwhile, Maggie
was shaking out the
queen costume so that
Kirsty could try it on. As she did, there
was another faint *pop*. Kirsty looked
around nervously. This
time, she saw the air
shimmer with a red
glow. Then the bow
and arrows on a
nearby Robin Hood
costume turned into
a set of bagpipes!

Kirsty's hand flew to her mouth. She hoped Maggie wouldn't notice the change. She had no idea how to explain why Robin Hood was now holding bagpipes!

She bit her lip as the earrings on a display to Maggie's left suddenly turned into pink-and-white striped candy. *The topaz must be inside something that Maggie is holding!* Kirsty thought.

Suddenly, she saw the goblin in armor step cautiously out of the window display. He had his visor open now, and his beady eyes were fixed on the costume in Maggie's arms. *Oh, no!* Kirsty thought. *The goblin must have seen the magic working, too.*

She watched anxiously as the goblin inched slowly toward Maggie. But, as he did, one of his big feet bumped into a container of plastic swords. The rattle made Maggie turn around.

Grabbing a sword, the goblin froze as if he was just another store display!

"Thanks for the costume," Kirsty said quickly, trying to distract Maggie. "Can I try it on now?"

Maggie looked at the suit of armor, puzzled, and turned back to Kirsty. "Of course," she replied. She helped Kirsty into the dress and draped the cape over her shoulders.

As Kirsty took the crown, she noticed a

huge golden stone in the middle of it. The stone seemed to shimmer and shine. Could it be the magic topaz? Kirsty put on the crown. Immediately, her head started to

tingle with fairy magic. "Oh, wow!" she breathed.

"Do you like it?" Maggie smiled. "I think I have a scepter in the stockroom that would look great with that costume. I'll see if I can find it for you."

As soon as Maggie had left, Kirsty looked for Rachel and Chloe behind the fairy display. "I have the topaz!" she called softly.

"Hooray!" Rachel exclaimed.

"Where is it?" asked Chloe, zooming out of Rachel's pocket in a whoosh of sparks.

"In the crown on my head!" replied Kirsty.

Rachel looked at Kirsty's head in surprise. "Crown?" she asked. "Do you mean the turban?"

Kirsty turned to look in the dressing room mirror. Immediately, she saw that the crown had changed into a turban! The golden topaz still glittered at its center. "It changed!" she breathed.

At that moment, Rachel let out a cry of alarm. "Kirsty!"

"Watch out!" Chloe exclaimed at the same time.

Kirsty whirled around to see that the goblin in armor had crept up on her while she wasn't looking. Cackling gleefully, he leaped forward and snatched the turban with the topaz right off Kirsty's head!

Stop That Goblin!

"I have the topaz!" the goblin shouted. He staggered through the store with the turban and its precious, glowing jewel.

"After him!" Kirsty cried. The goblin charged toward the entrance door, his metal armor clanking.

Rachel and Chloe raced after him.

"Come on!" the goblin in the red hat

shouted, running up the steps toward the door. But the armor wasn't easy for his friend to run in. The visor fell down over his eyes again, and he couldn't see anything! He bumped clumsily into the pile of Halloween buckets, sending them bouncing and rolling across the floor.

The goblin tripped over one of the buckets and lost his balance. "Whaaaa!" he cried, tumbling to the floor. As he fell,

the turban slipped from his hands and
flew through the air.

"You klutz!" the other goblin sputtered.
"What do you think you're doing?"

"I can't see," the armored goblin
whined, trying to pull his visor up. "And
now I've hurt myself!"

"Catch that turban, Rachel!" Kirsty
exclaimed as the turban flew through
the air.

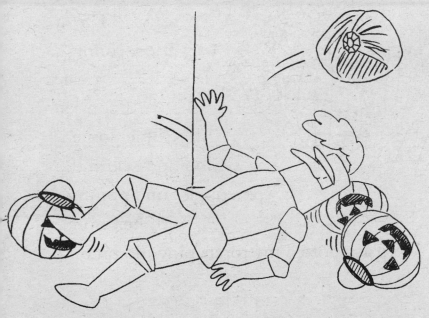

Rachel reached for it, but missed. As the turban hit the ground, the topaz was jolted out of its setting. The golden gem bounced across the floor and rolled in among the scattered buckets.

There was a loud *pop* and a shimmer of golden light. In the blink of an eye, all the pumpkins had changed into pineapples!

"Where's the topaz?" Kirsty cried, running over.

"I can see it!" Chloe gasped, swooping toward the pineapples and pointing with her wand.

Kirsty spotted the topaz glowing among

the fruit, too. But as Chloe zoomed
down to grab it,
the goblin by the
door also
spotted it.
He slid
through the
pineapples
as if he was
on ice and
scooped the
topaz up with
one hand just
before Chloe
reached it.

"Ow!" he
wailed as the heat
of the magic jewel
burned his icy goblin skin.

For a moment, Kirsty felt a glimmer of hope. She remembered that goblins couldn't touch the magic jewels with their bare hands. The jewels' magic burned them! She waited for the goblin to drop the topaz.

But instead, there was another loud *pop*. The goblin's costume and hat changed into a teddy-bear costume, complete with furry gloves that looked like paws!

"I have the topaz!" the teddy-bear
goblin shouted triumphantly to his friend,
who was scrambling out of his metal
armor. "Let's go!" Clutching the jewel
in his furry paws, he charged toward
the door.

Chloe swooped at the teddy-bear
goblin's head. "Give me back my jewel!"
she cried.

"No!" the goblin shouted. "The topaz isn't yours anymore. It's ours, and you're never going to get it back!"

"Come on, Kirsty!" Rachel cried. "We have to stop them!"

She and Kirsty began to run through the pineapples, trying not to trip. The goblins had reached the steps. They were going to get away with the topaz! But then, suddenly, Rachel had an idea. She picked up a pineapple as if it was a

bowling ball. With a thrust of her arm, she sent it rolling across the floor — right at the two goblins.

The pineapple hit the feet of the goblin who had been dressed in armor. He yelped in surprise and grabbed the arm of the teddy-bear goblin, who was halfway up the steps. For a moment, both goblins teetered on the steps, arms flailing. Then they toppled down the stairs and landed in a heap.

The topaz flew out of the goblin's furry paw and went spinning through the air. As it sailed past the lights, there was another *pop*. The air shimmered with an amber glow, and suddenly all the store lights became tiny disco balls that sparkled with magic.

Chloe raced after the jewel, and caught it in both hands. But it was too heavy for her to fly with. "Whoa!" she cried in alarm,

her wings fluttering frantically. She and
the jewel sank quickly
toward the ground.
"Help!"
Kirsty scrambled to
her feet and dived
for the fairy with her
hands outstretched.
Chloe and the Topaz
both landed safely
in her palms.
Kirsty pulled her
hands to her chest,
her heart beating fast.
Was Chloe OK?
"Phew!" Chloe said,
poking her head out
of Kirsty's cupped
hands and grinning.

"That was close. Thanks for catching me, Kirsty!"

"Are you all right?" Rachel asked, scrambling over and looking down at the fairy in concern.

"I'm fine," Chloe replied. Her hair was standing on end, but her brown eyes were sparkling. "In fact, I'm better than fine," she said, looking at the groaning goblins. "I have my topaz back!"

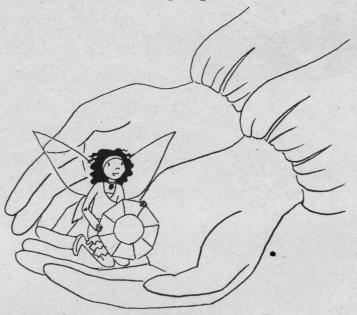

Just then, there was a noise from the stockroom. "I found the scepter!" Maggie called cheerfully. "I'll be out in a minute, once I put these boxes away."

"Oh, no!" Rachel gasped. "I forgot about Maggie." She looked around the store. There were pineapples all over the floor, glittering disco balls instead of lights, and pieces of armor scattered everywhere. Plus, the window display was ruined because its two mannequins were tangled in a heap by the door!

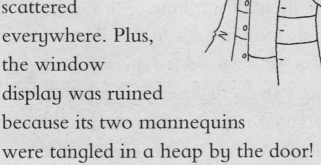

"Maggie will be really upset about this mess!" Kirsty said.

"Don't worry," Chloe replied cheerfully. "Now that I have the topaz back, I can work some changing magic." She touched her golden wand to the topaz in Kirsty's hand.

The tip of the wand began to gleam like a sparkling ray of sunshine. The little fairy lifted it high in the air and waved it expertly.

There was a quick series of *pops*, and everything started to change again. The air glimmered orange, then red, and finally gold. Then pineapples changed back to pumpkin buckets, the disco balls changed to normal lights, and two normal mannequins appeared in the window. Everything was magically back to how it had been in the first place! With a final *pop*, all the pieces of armor jumped neatly onto a shelf.

"Phew!" Rachel said in relief.

Chloe smiled at her. "It's all back to normal."

"Except for one thing," Kirsty said slowly. "What's Maggie going to say when she sees those goblins?"

Fluffy Bunnies

The goblins were picking themselves up
off the floor, groaning and arguing.
Their costumes had disappeared and they
were back to their ordinary green goblin
selves.

"Why did you trip me like that?" the
first goblin demanded.

"Why did you let go of the topaz?"

sputtered the other. "This is all your fault!"

"My fault? It's *your* fault!" the first goblin shouted.

"Oh, no. How are we going to explain those two to Maggie?" Rachel asked.

"Leave it to me!" Chloe flew over to the goblins.

"Pesky fairy!" snarled the first goblin, making a swipe at Chloe, who darted easily out of his way. "Give us back that topaz!"

"No," Chloe replied coolly. "And my wand is charged with changing magic now, so I can turn you into anything I want!" She smiled. "If you don't leave the store this minute, I'm going to turn you both into fluffy pink bunny rabbits!"

The goblins' mouths dropped open in horror.

"Bunny rabbits!" the first one exclaimed. "Yuck!"

"You wouldn't!" said the second.

Chloe grinned. "Oh, yes I would." She gave Rachel and Kirsty a mischievous look. "What do you two think?"

Rachel grinned back. "I think they'd make cute bunny rabbits," she said.

"Especially fluffy pink ones," Kirsty added.

Chloe lifted her wand.

"Noooooo!" both goblins cried in alarm. They turned and ran up the steps. Pushing and shoving, they yanked the door open and disappeared down the street as fast as they could run.

Rachel, Kirsty, and Chloe all burst out laughing.

"You girls seem to be having a good time," Maggie said, stepping out of the stockroom with a scepter in her hand.

Chloe darted into Rachel's pocket just in time.

"I'm sorry I took so long," Maggie added. She looked at the door, which was just swinging shut. "Have I missed a customer?"

"It's OK," said Kirsty, quickly putting the topaz back in her pocket. "It was just, er . . ."

"Someone looking for pineapples," Rachel finished quickly.

Kirsty hid a grin while Maggie looked at Rachel in surprise. "Pineapples?" she asked.

Rachel nodded. "When they realized you didn't sell any, they left," she added.

"Oh, how strange." Maggie blinked. "Well, never mind. Here's the scepter," she said, handing it to Kirsty. She turned

to Rachel. "Have you decided on your costume yet?"

"I think I'd liked to dress up as a fairy," Rachel replied. "You have some beautiful fairy wings and wands."

"Yes," Kirsty agreed, handing the scepter back to Maggie. "Thank you for letting me try on the costumes, but I think I'd like to dress up as a fairy, too." She saw Chloe's head pop out of Rachel's pocket. The fairy grinned and gave her a thumbs-up sign before quickly ducking back down.

Kirsty changed out of the queen costume and the girls each chose a pair

of wings and a wand. Just as they
finished paying for them, the phone rang.
"Enjoy your Halloween party, girls!"
Maggie said as she hurried off to answer
the call.

The moment she
disappeared, Chloe
flew out of Rachel's
pocket in a cloud of
fairy dust. "I wish I
could stay for your
party. I bet you'll
look great in your
fairy costumes! But
I'd better get back to
Fairyland now. Thank you
for helping me find the topaz."
Kirsty took the stone out of her pocket.

"Here it is," she said holding it out to the fairy.

Chloe touched her wand to the golden jewel. It disappeared safely back to Fairyland in a fountain of orange sparkles.

Rachel and Kirsty picked up their

shopping bags and headed out of
the shop.

"See you soon!" Chloe said as Rachel
pulled the door open.

"Bye!" the girls called. The little fairy
spun around in a swirl of golden light,
and then zoomed away.

"I'm so glad we were able to help her," Rachel said happily.

"Me, too," Kirsty agreed. A sparkle near the ceiling caught her eye, and she looked up. A single tiny disco ball was still hanging there, glittering and shining with fairy magic. "Look!" she exclaimed. "Chloe left one little disco ball behind."

Rachel laughed. "There will always be magic in the store now," she said. Then she spotted the bus turning onto Main Street. "Come on!" she gasped, pulling

the door closed behind them. "We have to catch the bus, Kirsty!"

They began to run down the street. "It's been an amazing day, hasn't it?"

Kirsty panted. "What do you think will happen tomorrow?"

"I don't know," Rachel said, as they reached the bus stop just in time and jumped on board the bus. She grinned at Kirsty. "But I bet it will be magical!"

RAINBOW magic™

THE JEWEL FAIRIES

Rachel and Kirsty have found the
jewels that belong to India, Scarlett,
Emily, and Chloe. Now they must look
for the jewel that has been stolen from

Amy the Amethyst Fairy!

Will they have any luck?
Join Rachel and Kirsty in this
special sneak peek. . . .

Ready for Adventure

"Kirsty, we're here!" Rachel Walker announced, looking out of the car window. She pointed at a large sign that read WELCOME TO TIPPINGTON MANOR.

Kirsty Tate, Rachel's best friend, was peering up at the cloudy sky. "I hope it doesn't rain," she said. Then the house caught her eye. "Oh, look, Rachel, there's the house! Isn't it beautiful?"

At the bottom of the long, sweeping gravel driveway stood Tippington Manor. It was a huge Victorian house with an enormous wooden door, rows of tall windows, and ivy climbing all over its old red bricks. The house was surrounded by gardens full of flowers and trees, their autumn leaves glowing in shades of red and gold.

"Look over there, Kirsty," Rachel said to her friend as Mr. Walker turned the car into the parking lot. "The Adventure Playground!"

Kirsty looked to where Rachel was pointing. She was excited to see the playground on a hill behind the house.

She glimpsed some tires dangling on ropes, a silver slide, and what looked like a big wooden treehouse in the center, built around a towering oak tree.

"Isn't it great?" Kirsty whispered to Rachel as they climbed out of the car. "The fairies would *love* that treehouse!"

Rachel grinned and nodded. She and Kirsty were lucky enough to be friends with the fairies! Whenever there was trouble in Fairyland, the two girls helped the fairies any way they could. They had already had lots of magical adventures, and they were sure there were more to come!

A fairy for every day!

The seven Rainbow Fairies are missing! Help rescue the fairies and bring the sparkle back to Fairyland.

When mean Jack Frost steals the Weather Fairies' magical feathers, the weather turns wacky. It's up to the Weather Fairies to fix it!

Jack Frost is causing trouble in Fairyland again! This time he's stolen the seven crown jewels. Without them, the magic in Fairyland is fading fast!

■SCHOLASTIC

www.scholastic.com

FAIRY1

Come flutter by Butterfly Meadow,
the new series by the creators of Rainbow Magic!

Butterfly Meadow #1: Dazzle's First Day
Dazzle is a new butterfly, fresh out of her cocoon. She doesn't know how to fly, and she's all alone! But Butterfly Meadow could be just what Dazzle is looking for.

Butterfly Meadow #2: Twinkle Dives In
Twinkle is feisty, fun, and always up for an adventure. But the nearby pond holds much more excitement than she expected!

Coming in June!

📖 **SCHOLASTIC**

www.scholastic.com

THERE'S ALWAYS AN ADVENTURE AT BIG APPLE BARN™!

When Happy Go Lucky, a young quarter pony,
is moved from his home to the stables at Big Apple Barn,
there's no telling what will happen.